First published in Great Britain in 2016 by Andersen Press Ltd.,
20 Vauxhall Bridge Road, London SW1V 2SA.
Originally published by Enchanted Lion Books, 351 Van Brunt Street,
Brooklyn, NY 11231, USA
Copyright © 2015, Enchanted Lion Books
Text copyright © 2015 by Michaël Escoffier
Illustrations copyright © 2015 by Kris Di Giacomo
Transfer of rights arranged through VeroK agency, Barcelona, Spain
The rights of Michaël Escoffier and Kris Di Giacomo to be identified
as the author and illustrator of this work have been asserted by them
in accordance with the Copyright, Designs and Patents Act, 1988.
Printed and bound in China.

10 9 8 7 6 5 4 3 2 1

British Library Cataloguing in Publication Data available.
ISBN 978 1 78344 482 3

WHERE'S THE BABOON?

written by Michaël Escoffier

illustrated by Kris Di Giacomo

Andersen Press

Who is the headmaster?

Who brought
an apple?

Who is hiding behind the castle?

Who made this painting?

Who can count to a **thousand?**

Who is copying the rabbit?

Who is the **Clown?**

Who is making
snowflakes?

Who is making mischief?

Who is playing with
the seagull?

Who left these droppings?

Who is having a
birthday?

Wait!
Who is missing?

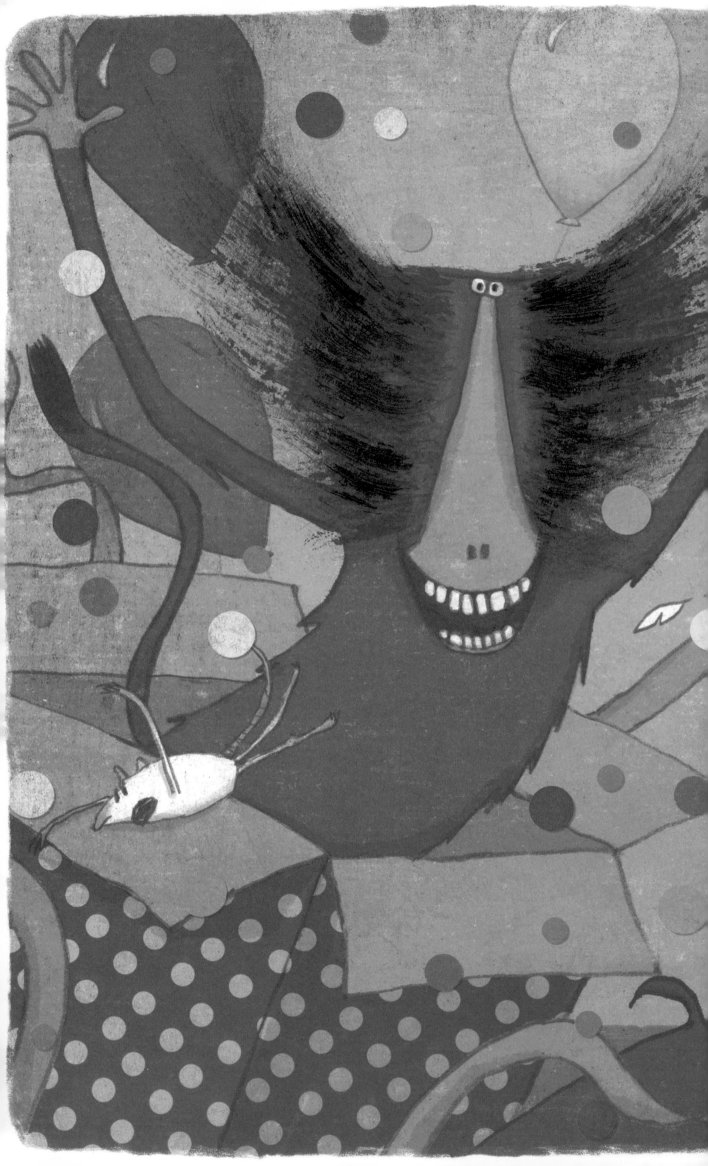